A Book to Read and Color

Adapted by
Suzanne Gruber

Illustrated by
Georgene Hartophilis

Watermill Press

Once upon a time, there were three little pigs.
They each left home to seek their fortunes.

FORTUNE
HOME

The first little pig met a man with bundles of straw.
"May I have some straw?" the pig asked.
"Sure," said the man.

The first little pig started building. In a short time, he had a nice house of straw.

Then a mean wolf came by and called,
"Let me in, let me in!"
"Not by the hair of my chinny
chin chin!" said the pig.

"Then I'll huff, and I'll puff, and I'll blow your house in!" cried the wolf.

The second little pig met a man with bundles of sticks.
"May I have some?" the pig asked.
"Sure," said the man.

The second little pig started building. In a short time, he had a nice house of sticks.

Then the wolf came by and called,
"Let me in, let me in!"

"Not by the hair of my chinny chin chin!" said the pig.

"Then I'll huff, and I'll puff, and I'll blow your house in!" cried the wolf.

The third little pig met a man with a load of bricks.
"May I have some?" the pig asked.
"Sure," said the man.

The third little pig started building. And after a long time, she had a nice house of bricks.

Along came the wolf. "Let me in, let me in!" he called.
"Not by the hair of my chinny chin chin!" said the pig.

"Then I'll huff, and I'll puff, and I'll blow your house in!" cried the wolf.

The wolf huffed and he puffed,
but he could not blow
the house in!

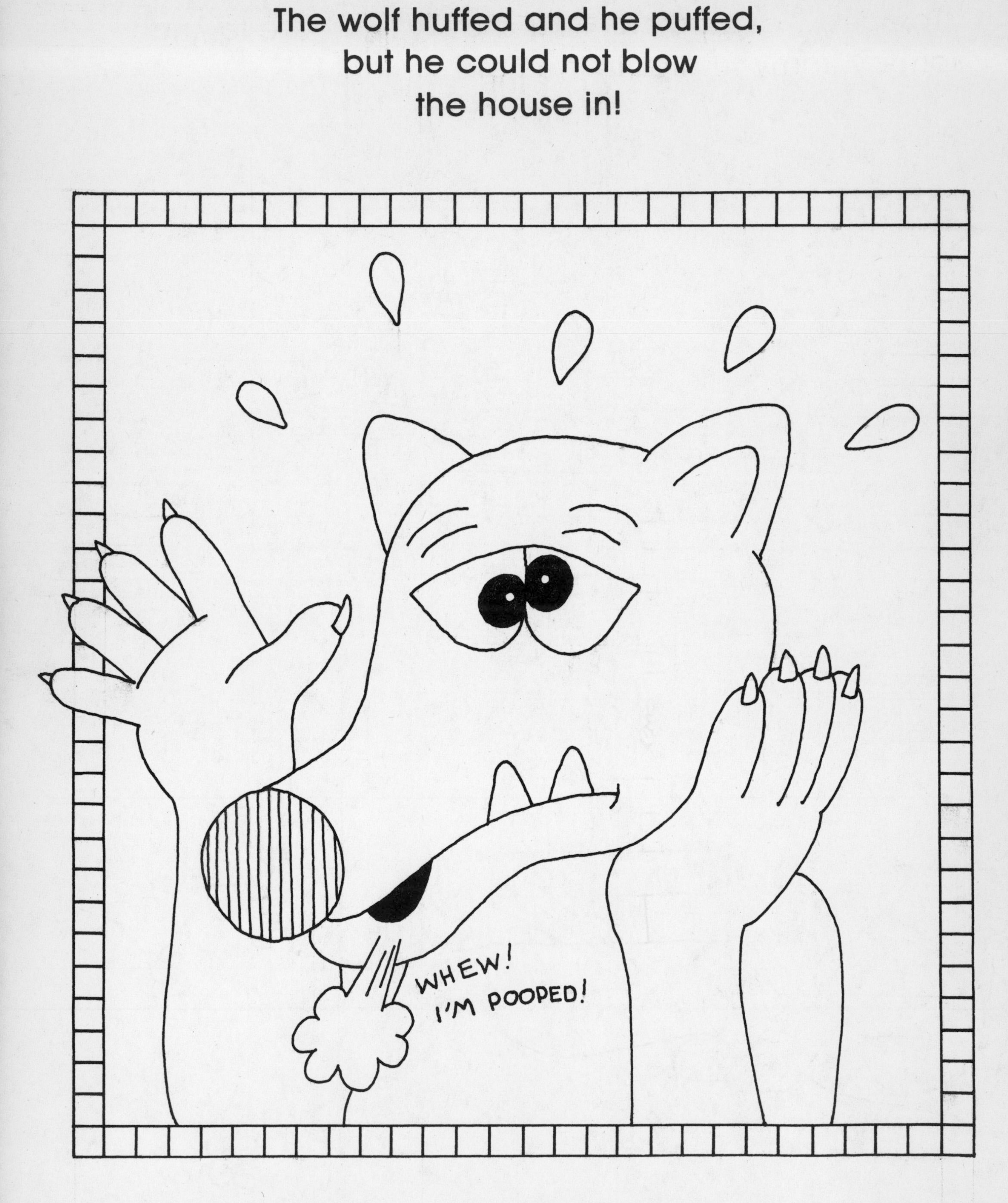

Then the wolf got a better idea. "Little pig," he called. "Tomorrow at six o'clock I'll show you where to find some yummy turnips in the field."

At five o'clock the next day, the pig went to the field by herself and found the turnips.

The wolf knocked on the pig's door
at six o'clock.
"I already have lots of turnips,"
the pig laughed.

The wolf thought of another idea. "Little pig," he called. "Tomorrow at five o'clock I'll show you where to find some juicy apples down the road."

At four o'clock the next day, the pig went down the road by herself and found the apples.

Suddenly, the wolf appeared.
"Why didn't you wait for me?" he asked.

"I have saved the best apple for you. Here it is," the pig said as she threw the apple.

While the wolf was chasing the apple,
the little pig ran home.

The next morning, the wolf said, "Little pig!
At three o'clock I'll take you to the fair in town."

As soon as the wolf went home, the little pig went to the fair by herself.

ICE CREAM

The wolf arrived at
three o'clock.
"I have already been
to the fair,"
the pig laughed.

The wolf grew very angry. He got a ladder and climbed up on the roof. "You have tricked me for the last time," he said. "Now I will come down your chimney!"

The little pig quickly built a fire in the fireplace.
Then she hung a huge pot of water over the fire.

Splash! The wolf came down the chimney and fell into the pot. The pig quickly put on the cover.

The little pig invited all her friends over for a party. And they all lived happily ever after.